BY

CORI LUKOMSKI

Tate Publishing, LCC

"This Is My Story" by Cori Lukomski

Published in the United States of America
by Tate Publishing, LLC
127 East Trade Center Terrace
Mustang, OK 73064
(888) 361–9473

ISBN: **1–5988620–4-9**

To God, my Father, be all the glory, honor, and praise

Acknowledgments

A great deal of thanks is due to a few individuals who have made this step of faith, not only possible, but also pleasant.

To my husband, Tim:
You have witnessed the events in this story first hand and have lovingly supported me through them all. Thank you so much for joining me in faithful submission to God's plan for our lives!

To my parents:
You introduced me to Jesus. I am eternally grateful for the awesome inheritance of your faith!

Table of Contents

A Note from the Author

When I came to you, brothers, I did not come with eloquence or superior wisdom as I proclaimed to you the testimony about God. For I resolved to know nothing while I was with you except Jesus Christ and him crucified. I came to you in weakness and fear, and with much trembling. My message and my preaching were not with wise and persuasive words, but with a demonstration of the Spirit's power, so that your faith might not rest on men's wisdom, but on God's power.
1 Corinthians 2:15

Dear Readers,

Over a year ago, God began leading me on an awesome journey of faith, and along the way, he asked me to put my testimony into writing. I do not know what God intends to accomplish through this story, but I know he has a good and perfect reason for bringing it into being. My soul overflows with love and gratitude that he might choose to use this book to bring about the same life change in another person that I have experienced. I encourage you to take each word to heart because, although it is written as fiction, this is truly my story. I have not added to or taken away from the spiritual elements to make them more interesting, attractive, or believable. I have simply attempted to convey the truth of God's interaction with our spirits and his desire for us to be in perfect communion with him through Jesus. At the end of the book, there is a section of short Bible studies entitled "See For Yourself" that I have included to help you delve further into God's Word. It is my hope and prayer that each person who reads these words will experience God's power in a new and life changing way.

Chapter One

(Summer 2004)

Blessed is the one who reads the words of this prophecy,
and blessed are those who hear it
and take to heart what is written in it.
Revelation 1:3

The woman sat quietly in the small sanctuary of the church as a large group of adolescents slowly trickled in the back doors, held up only by their widespread desire to socialize with one another. Peering at them discreetly out of the corner of her eye, the woman recognized that they were a typical group of today's youth. Most of the kids were dressed according to the standards set up by current pop culture. Wearing tops that were just a little too tight and revealing, the girls battled to be acceptable visual buffets for the boys who sported baggy shorts and t-shirts that displayed logos of the most fashionable brands in the mall. Playfully poking and pushing, they struggled to make their voices heard over one another by speaking as loudly as they could without hollering - although a few of them determined that it was necessary.

A few of the kids stood out as not fitting into the

social norm and, as a result, were not actively participating in the adolescent play. It was difficult to tell why these few stood apart from the group. Was it possible that their clothing did not meet the fashion standards that are so cruelly enforced by peer acceptance during the teen years, or were they too shy to keep up with the constant bantering that was taking place in the midst of the larger group? A small yet significant burst of hope welled up in the belly of the female observer. Maybe their exclusion was a result of their refusal to deny Christ in order to smoothly meld with their peers. This thought almost systematically led the woman's mind into memories of her earlier years when she too had battled to find her identity in a world that was intent upon destroying it.

Doubt settled in next to the hope inside her and acted as a bucket of cold water being poured onto the beginnings of a blazing fire. What was she thinking? How was she supposed to share the wisdom she had gained from living life with this rowdy group of kids? They were just going to think of her as old and out of style and dismiss the warnings and entreaties that she sent their way. What had she been thinking when she had contacted the youth minister of this impoverished, inner city church? She had never done anything like this before. She had no experience teaching on the spiritual realm. How could she have ever let God convince her she was capable of making a positive impact on these young people?

The woman closed her eyes tightly and sent up a desperate plea for help. *Father, help me to remember your promises! Help me to remember that I am simply allowing you to use me today! You have led me to this place, and although I am weak and insecure, Father, shine your light through me. Speak through me today and help me to glorify your name. I love you, and I trust you! Amen.*

A smile played with the corners of her mouth as she contemplated how cunning Satan was in his attempts to deter her from God's plan for her life and how quickly and resolutely her Father in Heaven put him in his place when she called on him for help. She mused at the fact that her relationship with the God of the universe had not made her immune to Satan's attacks and the pain of humanity. It had simply given her a place to go for relief and protection, and she rejoiced in the fact that, as their relationship developed, she was seeking God's guidance and protection more quickly in times of need. She could remember a time when she did not even consider asking for God's assistance until she was deeply entangled in Satan's snares.

As her thoughts wound down, the woman's eyes opened, and she scanned the room around her. She had been too nervous upon entering to take in the details of her surroundings. The church building itself was mostly nondescript. Block walls that had at one time been painted white held in rows of traditional, wooden pews softened with worn, red, upholstered cushions. Simple light fixtures hung from the cathedral style ceiling and aided the tall, narrow windows in illuminating the room. A pulpit sat on a raised, stage-like area at the front of the church with a single set of four stairs leading up to it, and on the wall behind the stage a large, decorative, wooden cross hung, proclaiming the passion that kept the church alive despite obvious hardship.

A crescendo in the noise produced by the adolescents drew her attention back to the rear of the sanctuary. A young man, probably in his early thirties, had joined the group and was attempting to herd it in the direction of the pews while joining in on its playful banter. He was of average height and weight and, quite honestly, average in every way except for the confident and loving manner in which he interacted with the kids. Identifying him as a probable candidate for the church's youth minister, the woman kept her eyes trained in his direction, hoping to make eye contact so she could introduce herself and let him know she was ready whenever he was. It did not take long for the contact to be made, and the man approached her with a warm, welcoming smile while the kids filed into the pews in a scattered format. He introduced himself and mentioned that he had a few matters of business to discuss with the group before she would begin her presentation. She settled back into the soft cushion of the pew and issued one final petition to God concerning the event that was about to transpire.

Chapter Two

Therefore let us leave the elementary teachings about Christ and go on to maturity, not laying again the foundation of repentance from the acts that lead to death, and of faith in God, instruction about baptisms, the laying on of hands, the resurrection of the dead, and eternal judgment. And God permitting, we will do so.
Hebrews 6:1-3

She heard the youth minister introducing her to the group, which was now surprisingly attentive considering its boisterous activity only moments before. Reluctantly cutting off her conversation with her Father in Heaven, she rose slowly and began approaching the front of the sanctuary. Undeniably, God had called her out of her comfort zone. She once again reminded herself that he would be faithful to sustain her through this act of obedient service while a thin layer of perspiration formed on her palms. As she made her way down the side aisle, she was keenly aware of the resounding click clack of her dress shoes on the age-worn wood floor, as well as the eyes of every teen in the group trained on her back. This sensation increased her discomfort, and she uselessly fought to keep the heat from rising to her cheeks.

Upon mounting the stairs that led to the pulpit, she dared to take a glance out at the conglomeration of adolescents that would soon be her audience. As she scanned the crowd, she read curiosity and interest in some eyes, while in others she saw the early onset of defiance and a hardened heart. No doubt many of these youngsters had already endured more in the few years of their lives than she had in over a quarter of a century. As if on cue, her mind replayed some of the telephone conversation she had with the youth minister when she arranged this engagement. "Before you commit to this, you need to understand the demographics of the youth population with which I work," he had said in a serious tone void of any condescension. "Many of these kids have been exposed to lives that are outside the range of our most wicked and tawdry imaginings. Combined with severe to moderate poverty, this sets up a situation that no human could completely overcome without the help of Jesus. Only a few are part of a family that encourages them to attend church, and more often than not, their friends and immediate family heckle them about their attendance. Although they are communicating an obvious search for something they are missing by their persistent attendance, they are still difficult to communicate seriously with unless you have previously built a relationship with them. To make matters more difficult, the relationship building aspect is no walk in the park either." He had made this last comment with a slight hint of humor born from experience. Once again Satan whispered softly in her mind. *"Your story won't impact these kids! They will laugh at your boring, uneventful life. How are you ever going to convince them that the spiritual darkness that you experienced as a pampered, middle class teen growing up in a Christian family is the same one that they battle daily?"* With a deep breath she expelled the thoughts, squared herself up with the pulpit where she had positioned her notes, and warmed her tense face with a smile.

In her nervousness she forgot the outline that lay before her and began with the first words that came to her mind. In a tight, shaky voice she said, "Looking around this sanctuary, I am reminded of the church I went to when I was growing up. I attended with my family every Sunday morning and night. I attended youth group and Vacation Bible School. I even went to church camp. When I was ten years old, I asked Jesus into my heart and was baptized because I realized that I was separated from God because of my sins, and I truly believed that God had sent Jesus to die on the cross to serve the punishment for the wrong things that I had done. I admit that I did not understand the entirety of that act, but I knew I loved Jesus because he had loved me enough to die in my place." Her eyes moistened at the memory of her pure, unquestioning faith as a child. Her smile broadened as her muscles relaxed, and the tension slowly loosed its grip on her body. It was quickly replaced with a passion that naturally flowed from a source deep within her soul. "Most people end their testimony at this point," she continued. "The moment Christ came to reside in their heart is the end of the story they tell, and we are left assuming that their life beyond that point must be a perfect example of Christianity or that asking Jesus to be a part of their everyday life alleviated all of the pain and hardship they had previously experienced." She paused here and scanned the audience to gauge their attention and understanding. Encouraged slightly by the observation of several nodding heads and eye contact with nearly every kid, she went on with her monologue. "My story begins at this common endpoint. I am here today to tell you how Jesus worked in my life after I asked him to become a permanent resident in my heart. I want to share with you the lessons that God has taught me and the ways he has grown me along the way. I want to tell you the story that led me to today."

Chapter Three

(Fall 1999)

He reached down from on high and took hold of me; he drew me out of deep waters.
2 Samuel 22:17

Darkness swaddled me tightly as I walked briskly across campus. A few dim security lights attempted to penetrate the night, but their beams could not reach the deep recesses of my soul. A crisp breeze along with the sound of dried leaves tripping about on the sidewalk verified that the fall season was in full swing. I normally reveled in these artistic details God had included in his creation, but tonight they simply intensified the spiritual agony through which I was trudging. Other than these sounds of the season and the consistent clomping of my athletic shoes on the pavement, the area surrounding me was silent. I was alone in my turmoil, more alone than I had felt in my entire lifetime.

This lonesome darkness that invaded my internal being was not only frightening, it was familiar. I recognized it from different times during my adolescent years when, in rebellion, I chose to turn from the God I had made amends with through Jesus as a child. During those times, I had quickly learned my lesson after being scathed by Satan's temptations and had crawled back to God in fear that he would not accept me again. There had been several times that the process had been elongated by the idea that I should perfect myself before presenting myself before my Maker. I would struggle hopelessly to be "good" and always fall short of what I presumed was God's expectation for me. Long ago I had realized that the quality of my relationship with God and the level this internal wattage that I could not quite explain were directly correlated. Although I had never seemed to be capable of keeping my soul consistently well lit, I was quite sure I preferred the light to the dark.

Fear washed over me as these memories flooded my brain, accompanied by a tightening of my throat that always indicated uncontrollable tears were on the way. I realized that the darkness that was settling in now might be permanent. I felt so utterly lost and confused. The foundation I had steadied my shaky, youthful soul on was potentially nonexistent, and I felt as if I were free falling through a pitch-black void. I ran over the questions in my mind hoping to find some assurance and certainty. *"How can the God of the Bible claim that Jesus is the only way to have a relationship with him and get to heaven?"* my professor's voice echoed. *"If God is a good and fair God like the Bible says he is, how can he condemn Hindus, Buddhists, Muslims and Jews to hell if they never knew about Jesus or really thought they were doing what God wanted by following their religion?"* This was just one of the many questions that had been posed in my religion class that whirled through my brain, casting doubt on everything I had based my life on up until this point.

I made an attempt to clear the slate in my mind and organize the facts and ideas that were spinning about. I knew without a doubt that somewhere in the Bible it said that God was just and he wanted all men to be saved. I was also confident that Jesus was quoted at some point in the Bible saying no man could get to the Father, meaning God, except through him. In addition to these two bits of knowledge, I was quite sure that it seemed awfully unfair to send people to hell who grew up having faith in a religion other than Christianity just because they had never had the opportunity to hear about Jesus, and what about the people who did hear about Jesus but would not turn their backs on the religion in which they grew up because they believed it to be the truth? It made sense that they would think their religion was right just like I had always thought mine was right. Most religions teach that it was the other way of thinking that was wrong for one reason or another.

Ugh! I wanted to scream! Tears had been coursing down my cheeks for quite some time now as I made my way through the tree-lined sidewalks that led to the campus library, and the profound silence was occasionally interrupted by a quiet sob that escaped from someplace deep inside me. I needed to study for my midterms. I did not have time for the mental traffic jam that was keeping my thoughts tied up in spiritual matters. Despite my frustration, my mind continued to wander as I slowed my pace, hoping to gain some type of composure before I neared the library where my temporary seclusion would be infiltrated by groups of students on their way to study in the protected quiet of the contemporary building. The thing that made these questions so terrifying was that I had always been told that the Bible was literally God's Word, and that God never lied or made a mistake. I knew these beliefs were based on actual words in the Bible, but unfortunately, I had never taken the time to commit them to memory. If I had discovered some contradictions that could not honestly and intellectually be explained, I felt like my basis for believing in God and my connection to him through Jesus Christ was a farce. As I neared my destination, I abruptly stopped on the path, not caring if anyone was around to witness my obvious emotional struggle. "God," I cried out in a ragged whisper. "I am so confused! I need to know if you are real! I need to know now because I cannot explain your existence or the Bible's truth in the face of all of these unanswered questions. I do not have to have the answers to the questions, but I need to know if you exist. If you just let me know you exist, I will not stop believing." My words trailed off haltingly mixed with sobs and sniffles. I remained planted in the spot in which I had sent up my urgent plea half expecting to be struck by lightening for questioning God in such a manner, but nothing happened, and after a few more seconds passed, I resumed my previous pace completing the remainder of my trek to the library in silence.

When I tugged open one of the heavy metal doors to the library, a burst of cool air hit my face, instantly communicating that the fleece pullover I had hastily stuffed in my book bag would be put to good use. I stepped into the open lobby and squinted my eyes as I walked to ward off the bright fluorescent lights until my pupils adjusted. Among the groups of whispering students clustered around tables, I recognized several faces, but I ducked my head quickly avoiding the social pleasantries necessary after eye contact. In order to manage the emotional and spiritual stress I was experiencing, as well as my literature and philosophy notes, I needed to be alone. I ascended the stairs to the second and then third floor of the library. Passing through aisles of dusty, book-covered shelves, I searched for a quiet, out-of- the-way study area. Without much trouble, I discovered a table with four chairs tucked into an alcove created by two bookshelves and a wall. I collapsed into one of the chairs with my back to the wall and dropped my book bag into the chair at my side. After a few moments of just sitting, I unzipped my bag and dug through it until I found my philosophy notebook.

Pulling it out, along with my fleece, I commenced my study session.

Although I had expected my mind to wander because of my spiritual confusion, I had little trouble attending to the material. I had decided to wait for God to make himself known if he existed. At first I had wondered if he would consider my plea a test and not respond even if he had heard, but it occurred to me that the God I had always believed in would know the condition of my heart and would follow through with a response if he truly did exist. I continued to study in the silence of my secluded corner of the library for nearly an hour before I was suddenly interrupted by a very human answer to prayer.

Looking up from my notes, I was caught in the gaze of a young man I recognized from my philosophy class. I had never spoken to him or learned his name. In fact, I could only remember a few times that he had actually attended class. At first I just looked at him and watched his lips move while his initial words resounded in my head. "Do you believe in God?" he had asked. No other introduction or interlude was given just the very abrupt, very timely words that shook me to the deepest depths of my soul. My mind rocked with confusion and fear. *How had he known I was struggling with that question? Had he seen me on campus? Was it a coincidence? Why was he approaching me with this in my hidden corner of the library? Should I answer his question and possibly engage in a conversation, or should I blow him off so he would leave me alone?* Then, a realization dawned in the dark, confused pit of my soul. It dawned in such way that the darkness that had been haunting me was pierced with a refreshing stream of light that banished the fear and confusion and replaced it with an unexplainable peace. I realized that this person was the answer to my prayer whether he realized it or not. God had heard my plea for help. He had recognized my need and supplied it in the most natural manner. He had sent this boy with whom I was familiar into this common, college hangout simply to let me know that he heard my petition and therefore, he existed. How was I so sure? I recognized the light. I recognized the peace and assurance. None of my professor's questions had been answered in that moment, but I knew in my soul that God existed even though I did not know all of the answers. I had the only proof that I needed to establish the reality of my Father in Heaven - the intangible, warm glow of his eternal light. I had known it before, but I had never recognized it for that which it truly was, the proof that man continually seeks for God's existence. How I clung to the lifeline that my Father threw to me that night. I had nearly given my soul over to eternal death, but in one loving gesture he lifted his child from the darkness.

I reveled in the unexplainable security I felt in that knowledge as I focused in on the young man who stood before me. In a shaky, breathless voice I said, "You are never going to believe this, but you are an answer to a prayer I said tonight." He sat down across from me while I delved into the events that had occurred that evening and the ones that had led up to them, and I realized during our conversation that I had been wrong. He did believe my story, and miraculously, I did too.

Chapter Four

(Summer 2004)

"For my thoughts are not your thoughts, neither are your ways my ways," declares the Lord. "As the heavens are higher than the earth, so are my ways higher than your ways and my thoughts than your thoughts."
Isaiah 55:8–9

Silence filled the small sanctuary as she focused in on her audience. She had gradually lost herself in the memories and emotions from her past while she spoke. Now she paused while she looked out at the teenagers, hoping to gauge their response to this monumental spiritual event from her life. Although the majority of the assemblage projected moderate interest in the words she had spoken, she was not satisfied with the overall response. She lifted a quick entreaty to God for his power to work through her to touch the lives of the young people to whom she spoke, and then began to expound on her story.

"I had spent nearly my entire Christian life, up until that point, knowing about God and Christianity but not truly developing or even understanding faith. What my child-like faith had begun when I was ten had been infiltrated by human, therefore faulty, knowledge and wisdom. I had only believed as far as my human understanding would allow me to go, and when I was faced with something I was not able to comprehend, I was forced to make a decision about whether the God that I chose to believe in when it was easy to trust was worth taking a chance on even when I could not understand everything that he was doing. That is when I first truly understood the meaning of faith. I realized that faith is believing and trusting in something even though it is beyond our complete understanding."

She took in a long, slow gulp of air to steady her breathing. She was frustrated because it seemed like she was talking in circles and that none of her thoughts connected. How was she going to express the immense treasure she had found in this one little nugget of wisdom? A comforting reminder resounded in her head. God could work through her ineptness. In fact, the idea that he could accomplish anything through her feeble efforts proved his incomprehensible power and might. The verse in 2 Corinthians from which this truth came flashed through her mind. *"But we have this treasure in jars of clay to show that this all-surpassing power is from God and not from us (4:7–9–NIV)."* She knew that was why she was here fumbling through her spiritual journey in front of these kids with whom she was not confident she could relate. God had brought her here to this place to accomplish something that she could only do through his power.

Hoping to further engage her audience, she decided to pose a question to the young adults. She left the protection of the pulpit and descended the platform stairs in order to achieve a more intimate feel during the approaching discussion. In a voice that resounded with her renewed confidence she asked, "Have you ever been in an situation that tempted you to question God's power or maybe even his existence?"

She received no response, so she continued in a gentle voice. "Have you ever heard someone say that God cannot possibly exist because of all the bad things that happen in the world or because of some biblical detail that cannot be explained with physical proof?" A scattering of timid hands rose from the gathering of adolescents. "Have you ever wondered if the person was right because you could not counter his or her argument with logical explanations that annihilated any remnant of doubt?" Several hands quickly dropped, but a few persevered in their honest admission of uncertainty.

"In the first chapter of 1 Corinthians Paul explains the quality of our human wisdom by saying, 'For the foolishness of God is wiser than man's wisdom.'" With a smile gracing her face she said, " I think this is probably pretty self-explanatory, but just in case, I will explain. Our best and brightest human wisdom does not even measure up to God's simplest thoughts. We are not qualified to tell God what makes sense and what does not because there is no possible way we can understand his thinking and actions. Even when we do not understand God's ways we should still choose to trust in his wisdom that is so much greater than our own. In fact, Paul also tells us in 1 Corinthians that this inability to understand God completely was all a part of God's master plan. Paul states, 'For since in the wisdom of God the world through its wisdom did not know him . . . ' In other words, God created us so we had to either come to him through faith or not at all." She allowed a few seconds to slip by without speaking, hoping to allow the truth of God's Word to seep into the young souls that she was entertaining. "You see, when I was ten years old I simply had faith in God and his Word. As a result, I was able to have a close relationship with him because of my acceptance of his forgiveness through Jesus, but as I grew older I gradually accumulated human wisdom. As I matured and was educated I began to think that I was wise. In fact, as embarrassing as it is to admit, there is an entry in one of my old journals in which I was audacious enough to put that thought into writing." This admission elicited a few chuckles from the crowd. "Unfortunately, the smarter I thought I was, the further I pushed myself away from God until the day I nearly separated myself from him completely. I am thankful that God is a merciful and faithful God who does not back out on his promises, and he was there reaching out to me when I cried out to him from the dark pit I had fallen into."

During these last few statements her voice was choked with the emotion that resided in these memories as she realized all over again how awesome God's love was for her - that he would continue to stand by her side through years of self-centered, prideful behavior. In only a few moments she had gained control of her emotions and continued by saying, "I hope that none of you will ever allow the limited capabilities of your human understanding to keep you from experiencing the amazing love of God for yourself." She was turning to head back up the platform so she could continue with the aid of her notes when God placed an overwhelming desire on her heart to lead the group in prayer. Before she could even reach the first step, she turned back to face her audience. "Although this might seem like an odd time to do this, I think we need to pray. I feel like there might be some here who have never accepted Jesus' sacrifice for the forgiveness of their sins, and as a result, they have not been able to have a personal relationship with God. I am going to pray a prayer that you can say to God to begin this life-changing relationship. If you know this is a decision that you want to make right now, all you have to do is follow along with me, or you can talk to God in your own words. If this is a decision you have already made, please pray that your friends would be open to God's love and accepting of his forgiveness through Jesus Christ."

She watched and waited as all of the teenagers bowed

their heads and some of them clasped their hands together before she bowed her own head and began. "Father, I know that I sin and that this separates me from you. I also believe that you sent Jesus to earth to pay the price for my sins on the cross. I want to accept that undeserved, sacrificial gift today so that I can be in a personal relationship with you. Thank you for your faithful love. Amen." When her prayer was over, she looked out over the group of teenagers that were before her. She noticed several faces were wet with freshly shed tears and a few individuals who where still bent over in prayer. Hoping to give everyone a few minutes to finish their private conversations with God, she turned and finished her walk up to the podium. Waiting for the last few heads to pop up, she shuffled through her notes, trying to find the best place from which to commence. She had strayed slightly from her prepared presentation, so it took her several seconds to locate the correct location on her outline. When she finally looked up, she saw that the young audience was waiting expectantly for her to continue.

"Once we have begun a personal relationship with God, he wants us to continue growing spiritually. He does not want our spirit to remain infantile, so he continually provides us with opportunities for growth. Some of them are not necessarily pleasant at the time, but they lead to an unfurling of God's good and perfect plan in our lives. Of course, like in most other things, God allows us to choose whether we are going to accept the opportunities he gives us to grow. Unfortunately, it took a long time after I initiated a relationship with God before I chose to grow through the opportunities that he placed before me, but once I began to mature I realized that I was starving to know my Father in Heaven better. I asked God to reveal himself to me and to accomplish his will in my life, and that launched a period of spiritual growth and maturation that testifies to the power of God."

Chapter Five

(Fall 2001)

In that day they will say, "Surely this is our God; we trusted in him, and he saved us. This is the Lord, we trusted in him; let us rejoice and be glad in his salvation."
Isaiah 25:9

My mind wondered blissfully from one thought to another as I walked briskly along the sidewalk with the heat from the early September sun making my skin sticky with sweat. I had walked this route every morning during the summer, and it had provided me with a wonderful pocket of time to brainstorm about the day ahead or contemplate decisions that I needed to make. Today I was simply taking in the beauty of the approaching autumn season and thanking God for blessing my life so richly with undeserved joy. My soul literally felt like it could burst and shower my surroundings with the overwhelming contentment that satiated my inner being.

A refreshing breeze meandered through the air and tickled the tree branches above my head, creating a rustling accompaniment for the twittering birds as my thoughts became a slide show of all the wonderful things with which God had blessed me during my nearly 21 years of life: parents and a new husband who loved and supported me, good health, opportunities to travel, a good education, and most recently, God had continued to answer my prayers for continued growth by revealing his character and his will to me in a variety of ways. My mind wandered slightly from the topic of blessings to consider what life event God might choose to grow me through next. *Would it be another disappointment turned into a beautiful lesson or simply an inspiring Bible study at church?* As quickly as the quandary had burst into my train of thought it receded to the back of my mind and was replaced with more musings about the beauty of the day.

My blissful thoughts were rudely interrupted by the sound of traffic as I approached a busy intersection near the university I attended. I kept my eye on the traffic light, hoping it would change to stop the speeding vehicles before I reached the corner. Unfortunately, my timing was off, and I had to wait impatiently for several moments on the dirty, litter-strewn curb until the light cooperated. As soon as the traffic screeched to a halt, I took off across the cross walk with my mood only slightly tempered by the inconvenience of the light. Hoping to make up the few wasted seconds, I increased the speed of my pace as I began walking along the shaded campus sidewalks that wound along under a canopy of ancient trees.

Without much concern, I noticed that the two city blocks that contained the university grounds were uncommonly empty and quiet, especially for such a beautiful early autumn day. There were no students bustling to their mid-morning classes or professors sauntering along the paths enjoying steaming cups of coffee despite the sun's warmth that was sneaking through openings in the protective barrier formed by the trees above. As I neared the administration building, I noticed a rather rotund young man who appeared to be near my age approaching from the opposite direction.

Although it was difficult to tell from my location, he seemed to be somewhat troubled and was nervously glancing about as he waddled toward some unknown destination. Hoping to share some of the excess happiness I was experiencing, I allowed a full, toothy smile to spread across my face as I reached him on the path. To my surprise, he did not seem to appreciate my joyous expression. In fact, in a rather curt manner he said, "Haven't you heard?" Based on my puzzled expression, he assumed I had not and continued in a somewhat more civil but no less tense voice, "New York City is under attack and nobody knows what is happening!" As if he had no more time to waste, he scurried off as quickly as he could carry his oversized body toward what I assumed he believed to be a more secure location.

I stared after the young man for a few moments not quite knowing how to react to his bizarre behavior and anxious statement. Slowly, I resumed my pace contemplating the peculiar occurrence. *Was New York City under attack? If so, by whom?* My thoughts floated around these and other similar questions for about a quarter of a mile, but gradually, my beautiful, not to mention peaceful, surroundings took center stage in my mind and warded off any concern that might have developed from the news.

When I arrived home, I was immediately welcomed by the persistent beeping of the answering machine. My eyes fell to the digital screen, which indicated I had received eleven calls during my forty-five minute walk. Pushing the play button, I initiated an onslaught of calls from family and friends inquiring about the location of my husband and I, asking if we had heard what had happened, and requesting that we return the calls as soon as we got the messages. At this point, the short-lived curiosity that I had experienced after the strange encounter on campus emerged in a more attention grabbing form. I picked up the television remote and pushed the power button. Pictures of fire, smoke, falling buildings, and terrified people immediately filled the screen. I listened to reporters, who were tucked away safely in newsrooms, narrate the scenes that flashed on the television. Now the nervous actions and tense voice of the young man on campus seemed a little more sensible.

As I continued to watch the breaking news, I picked up the phone and called my husband's work place to see if he had heard the reports and to make sure nothing out of the ordinary had happened at his location. Once I was assured of his safety, I began contacting the friends and family who had seemed so distressed on the answering machine. One by one, I reached them in an attempt to convince them that I was out of harm's way. I was immediately aware that most of the individuals with whom I spoke were nearly incapacitated by their fear. As our conversations progressed, I wondered why the morning's events had not filled me with overwhelming dread, and then, as I ventured to comfort the individuals with whom I spoke, I realized, or rather God revealed, the factor behind this dissimilarity.

From somewhere deep within my being the revelation resounded in crisp, clear tones, *"I have a hope!"* My soul swelled at the thought. I was not afraid because I knew that whatever the circumstances were I was secure in my relationship with God through Christ Jesus. Even if I lost my physical life in this moment of national chaos and confusion, I knew that I had the promise of eternal life with God in Heaven. This hope had not been attained by anything I had done but only by my belief and acceptance of the sacrificial act of Christ dying for the sins of the world. Tears of elation flowed down my cheeks as I realized that God had grown me, a woman who had once doubted God's existence, to a point in which I had assurance of my salvation. Praise to my

Father in Heaven for the awesome work that he was accomplishing in me poured from my lips as I slid to the floor in complete submission to my God.

As I sat on the floor, the phone abandoned beside me and adoration flowing from me, God shared another more sobering reality with me. He laid it heavily on my heart that this hope was not for me alone. Through the tragedy on this bittersweet, September morning, God not only made me aware of the hope I possessed, but he had introduced me to several individuals that I loved who did not share the same hope. Shame washed over me as I realized how long I had known these people and how many opportunities I had allowed to pass by without sharing the good news about Christ. Like a soft, yet persistent whisper, a convicting thought arrested my attention. *Who am I to keep this hope as my secret treasure?*

There in my tidy little living room, surrounded by hand-me-down furniture and family photographs, God commissioned me to share the message of Christ with those who did not possess the hope he gives so freely. I eagerly embraced this new mission, warding off any doubt in my ability to perform this awesome task by remembering the promise made in Philippians 1:6, "that he who began a good work in [me] will be faithful to complete it."

Chapter Six

(Summer 2004)

Do not conform any longer to the pattern of this world, but be transformed by the renewing of your mind. Then you will be able to test and approve what God's will is - his good, pleasing, and perfect will.
Romans 12:2

As the second account from her life culminated, she scanned the group of adolescents that sat before her with varying degrees of understanding and interest reflected on their faces. She was grateful that none of the few who silently expressed boredom and disinterest chose to distract those who were choosing to listen with some level of attentiveness. With amazement in how God was using her to impact this group of young people, she realized that her spiritual story, no matter how tame and uneventful, was speaking to the hearts of these kids whom God had brought to this worn out building to hear her speak. Glancing at her carefully prepared notes that had turned out to be less necessary than she had expected, she commenced with the monologue that she had prepared.

"The next years of my life did not unfurl as you might have expected. God gave me a glimpse of what he had in store for me on that infamous morning three years ago, but he knew I was not quite prepared for the work he had for me to do. He spent the days and months that have passed since that moment of revelation to grow me in knowledge and in truth and to prepare me for the specific tasks he had created me to accomplish in his kingdom." Streams of mid-afternoon sun shone through the clear glass windows of the sanctuary while she spoke, exposing streaks that had probably been created as some loyal volunteer had painstakingly washed the tall windows while teetering on the steps of a ladder. The rays warmed the room as the woman briefly detailed the ways in which God had changed her heart and opened her eyes to his truth.

"I graduated from the university the following year with an idealistic heart and a determination to serve God greatly in my chosen profession. Almost immediately, I was offered a position at the school of my choice, and without a moment's hesitation, I accepted. I felt that this inner city school was the perfect place to serve God by sharing his love with children who were starved for love in every other area of their life. Of course, I realized as a teacher I would not actually be able to tell them about Jesus or speak to them about my relationship with God, but I felt that just loving them with the love God had put in my heart would be enough to spur them on to seek out the source of that love elsewhere. I was quite confident that this was a life plan that would honor God.

A smile tickled the corners of her mouth just enough to give way to the telltale dimples in each of her cheeks as she made these statements. "Now," she said, "I am sure that you can already see some flaws in my logic, starting with the fact that it was my logic. I thank the Lord everyday for his patience because you would think, by this point, I would have figured out that I should seek God's wisdom concerning huge life decisions rather than trust my own judgment, but obviously, this lesson had not quiet penetrated my thick skull. Fortunately, God's plans are not thwarted by our slowness to understand and act upon his truth. In fact, he uses our mistakes to help us learn spiritual lessons that bring us closer to becoming the people he intended us to be.

I spent the next year teaching middle school students about math, reading, and most importantly, good character. God faithfully answered my prayers to put his love for each child into my heart, and each day I poured that love out on them through every possible channel. I diligently worked to instill in my students the desire to be their best and the knowledge that I loved and accepted them even when they were not. Investing all that I had - my time, my money, my knowledge, and my love - I persevered through a year of moderate success and limited reward. Believing that an individual's spirit would be at peace in spite of her situation if she was doing the will of God, I was confused by the unhappiness, frustration, and misery that continued into my second year, and I prayed that God would reveal the source of my dissatisfaction. Never having time for anything but work, I neglected the two things that I desired to have as my top priorities, my relationship with God and my family. As a result, I became even more frustrated and despondent. I was not sure how any of this could possibly be what God had planned for my life, but every time my thoughts went in that direction, I reminded myself of what Jesus had endured for me on the cross to fulfill God's plan and decided I could endure the small discomforts of this job to accomplish God's will for my life."

Chapter Seven

(Winter 2003)

For the word of God is living and active. Sharper than any double edged sword . . . it judges the thoughts and attitudes of the heart.
Hebrews 4:12

"At what point did you determine that this was God's will?" The question stormed to the forefront of my mind as I reread the familiar verse off of the jumbo screen in the sanctuary. Tears had been streaming down my face since the beginning of the worship service. Over the last few months my husband had gotten used to this type of emotional display and sat beside me as if nothing were the matter. I was thankful for his momentary lack of involvement because I needed this time to listen to God and contemplate what his Holy Spirit was attempting to communicate with me. For months I had been praying for deliverance from the bleakness that haunted my soul, and now, God's Word communicated the answer to those prayers. Again, I scanned the verse that loomed before me in bold, black letters on the stark, white background. "My father, if it is possible, may this cup be taken from me. Yet not as I will, but as you will." The verse was immediately followed by its Biblical address,

Matthew 26:39.

Like a throbbing heart the question continued to drum out its beat in my mind and in my soul, taunting me with Jesus' words. *"Yet not as I will, but as you will."* Realization was accompanied by dismay as the answer to the question became clear, but dismay quickly gave way to relief, as I finally comprehended the source of the persistent misery that had dogged the heels of my career. In an act of absolute self-absorption I had simply assumed I knew what God's will would be and had acted upon it. I had never taken the time to ask him *how* he wanted me to share his love with others. Instead of trusting in God to map out my life, I had charged ahead forging paths and mapping out my own course based on my own abilities and judgment. I shook my bowed head in disgust as tears took a curving path to the tip of my nose where they paused momentarily before dropping onto my already damp lap. I had spent months enduring the torturous stress of my teaching position while repeating over and over to myself that I could stick with this if Jesus could die on the cross for me when the entire time I had missed this Scripture's key application to my situation. I was not submitting to God's will. Instead, I had imposed my will on God, and I had subsequently suffered at my own hand. Unfortunately, there was no blessing in my agony because I had ultimately been serving myself rather than God.

Sorrow filled my soul as I mourned the time I had wasted and the manner in which I had dishonored my Father in Heaven with my prideful spirit. Simultaneously, I praised God for answering my prayers and for continuing to patiently guide me through life. I did not know if the goose bumps that covered my flesh were caused by the overuse of the air conditioning in the sanctuary or the undeniable presence of God's hand working in my life at that moment. I was filled with the knowledge that I was under spiritual construction as God built upon the foundation he had laid so many years before in his perfect wisdom. This knowledge brought an indescribable sense of security and peace into my soul as the service concluded. Knowing that God was going to take care of the details of my life allowed my weary soul to rest in humble submission to his perfect plan.

In that moment I knew that I simply needed to seek God's will for my life and patiently wait for his response before I reacted in any way to this new revelation. He already had a plan for me that was greater than anything I could independently create, so for the first time in my life, I would wholly trust in God's design for my life instead of my own. I exhaled deeply as the closing notes of a contemporary gospel chorus played out. I raised my bowed head and looked into the concerned eyes of my loving husband. A small smile spread across my lips that generated somewhere deep inside my newly peaceful soul. In a soft voice I assured him that everything was going to be all right and caught his hand in mine as I rose from my seat, signaling that I was ready to exit.

As we walked away from the church, I smoothed the wrinkles out of my tear-stained clothes. Peeking from behind grey clouds that threatened more snow, the sun attempted to warm the earth, but instead, in combination with the snow covered ground, it created a blinding glare. With my eyes squinted and snow crunching beneath my feet, I contemplated the new wisdom God had shared with me. I realized that I possessed a new understanding of my situation and my relationship with God. Although it was hazy and unclear, I grasped onto this knowledge, realizing that it would take me another step closer to becoming the person God intended me to be. Anticipation filled my heart as my husband maneuvered our late model car through the holiday traffic. *Where was God leading me? What was God's good and perfect plan for my life?*

The next morning I grudgingly awoke to the blaring of my alarm clock. In protest I flung my arm blindly in the direction of the unwelcome sound, attempting to hit the snooze. Instead, my hand grazed the edged of the annoying device and sent it tumbling off the nightstand. Although this was not my original plan of action, it accomplished my goal, and the crass noise that had rudely interrupted my sleep immediately abated. Unfortunately, after the physical exertion of the event I was completely awake, not to mention the fact that the cold air from the room had gained access to the cozy chamber I had made between the blankets. Pulling the covers more tightly around me, I attempted to regain my previous state of bliss, but it was impossible. As I lay there snuggling between the covers fighting off the realization that I had to get up, I replayed the events from the previous day in my mind. After I had gotten used to the idea that I had been chasing after a falsified version of God's will for the past five and a half years while bumbling along to the beat of my own drum, I had spent some time contemplating how I was going to learn God's true will for my life. For the first time in my Christian life, I realized that I wanted to know what God had to say about my situation. I was tired of trying to anticipate his responses to my questions, which always seemed to result in a mess. I prayed. It was not a long, elaborate monologue but a simple entreaty that required an eventual response, and I waited. Without much of a lapse in time, the Holy Spirit reminded me that the Bible is not referred to as God's Word without reason, and with God's guidance I made the commitment to him and myself to seek out his will through daily prayer and the study of his Word.

As if the episode with the alarm clock had not awoken my husband from his slumber, I stealthily slipped from between the sheets, tiptoed across the room, and slowly opened the bedroom door, hoping to avoid the all too common squeak that generally accompanied its movement. Happy that I had been able to vacate the room with not so much as a change in the rhythm of my husband's snoring, I made my way to our home office to keep my appointment with the Creator of the Universe. I sat down in the cushioned desk chair and picked my Bible up from the pile of books sitting unused on the nearby bookshelf. Upon opening the neglected book, I half expected a cloud of dust to send me into a fit of sneezing that would be the final undoing of my husband's restful sleep. To my surprise the crisp, white pages fell open without the accusation of a single flying dust particle.

Not knowing exactly where to begin, I prayed silently that God would teach me his will for my life through the Scripture I read, and deciding to begin where the pages had fallen open, I delved into the book of James. *"Consider it pure joy, my brothers, whenever you face trials of many kinds, because you know that the testing of your faith develops perseverance. Perseverance must finish its work so that you may be mature and complete, not lacking anything. If any of you lacks wisdom, he should ask God, who gives generously to all without finding fault, and it will be given to him." (James 1:2–5)* Without interlude, God breathed a soothing balm into my aching soul through these first verses that my eyes hungrily devoured. I heard his voice. I felt his presence. I basked in his love. For the first time in my Christian life I experienced the Bible as the living Word of God. I realized that this book was not a history book with recordings of Jesus Christ's life or an inspiring storybook with wonderful life lessons, but a treasured device for communication between my Father in Heaven and I. He literally communicated with my soul that morning with messages that applied to my specific life situation. I felt his guidance and I knew his will for that moment, so I persevered in prayer and the study of his Word, daily asking for his wisdom for my life.

Chapter Eight

(Summer 2004)

Their land is full of idols; they bow down to the work of their hands, to what their fingers have made.
Isaiah 2:8

Disbelief shadowed the eyes of many of the teens in the audience. She had known that this concept would be difficult to grasp. Somehow, God was easy to take as long as he was perceived as distant and inactive, but as soon as it was mentioned that he might literally be involved in the lives of his children, the skeptics arose. Realizing that this was one of the many things only God could inspire the human soul to understand, she silently requested the Holy Spirit to clarify her message as it was heard by the young people who sat before her.

As her supplication made its way to the ears of her Heavenly Father, she once again descended the stairs in an attempt to gain a more intimate audience with the crowd. Making eye contact with each person as she scanned the current pew inhabitants, she continued her oratory. "It is important to understand that there are some lessons that only God can teach our souls. Recognizing that God can communicate with us through his Word is one of those occurrences of which humans can speak, but only God can explain. As a result, I want you to know that it is not my intention to convince you of the reality of my previous statements because I know that is something only God can do, but I do wish to encourage you to delve into the Bible in a way that would allow him to introduce you to the life that exists in the sacred pages of his Word."

Witnessing an immediate release of tension from the group of teenagers that were gathered before her, she smiled in response to the Holy Spirit's timely reply. Knowing they were now comfortable enough with the idea to hear her out, she continued with her story. "You see, for nearly six months I faithfully spent time with God each day, reading his Word and praying for him to reveal his will to me. During those months, I was often plagued with doubt and confusion, but God's holy light continued to guide me past the darkness that threatened to invade my life along the narrow path that led to his ultimate will. I consciously chose to trust in God's promises. His Word told me that if I asked for his wisdom he would give it to me, so I asked and believed he would. Anytime that Satan tried to convince me that God was not listening or that I was wasting my time, the Holy Spirit reminded me of God's faithfulness in past situations and encouraged me to remain steadfast.

Finally, as the world around me began to unfurl into the new life that Spring unleashes, I realized what God was asking of me. Cutting through the bones and marrow of who I had portrayed myself to be, God's Word had revealed the true thoughts and attitudes of my heart. I had pridefully clung to my title and profession to validate my personal worth. I had selfishly planned to store up treasures on earth trusting in the financial security that my job provided, and I had skillfully crafted an idol of my work, allowing nothing else to have priority over it. In a clear and resounding voice the Holy

Spirit counseled me to validate myself through my status as a child of God, to store up my treasure in heaven rather than on earth, and to put God above all else in my life. Although I had heard these ideas with my mind many times during my life, this was the moment that God spoke them to my heart. I was at a crossroads. This was my time to choose between a relationship with God that was everything that it was meant to be and a shallow, hypocritical relationship that only existed on the exterior of my life but resulted in no true life change.

These bits of godly wisdom and guidance had been revealed over a period of many months and finally culminated in the midst of an unseasonably warm spring weekend. I sat down with my husband to watch television after a spirited game of catch in the backyard on that seemingly inconsequential Sunday afternoon, and with sweat still glistening on my brow, I shared the ways in which God had challenged me to trust him completely and entirely submit my life plans to him. Before venturing into this conversation, I had lifted it up to God earlier in the day, asking him to share the same spiritual vision with my husband, so it would not become a rift in our marriage. God had led me to do this during my morning Bible study through the story of Mary and Joseph. When Mary mysteriously became pregnant, God sent an angel to explain the occurrence to Joseph, so he would understand God's will in the situation. In the same manner God was faithful to me. My husband did not exhibit a moment's hesitation in his support and encouragement of me following God's guidance."

She paused momentarily before making her next statement. "Now, my husband's cheerleading might not seem like that significant of a gesture compared to Joseph accepting Mary's unexpected pregnancy, and maybe it is not. However, I have not yet disclosed to what extent God was asking me to trust him.

Chapter Nine

(March 2004)

But the man who looks intently into the perfect law that gives freedom, and continues to do this, not forgetting what he has heard, but doing it - he will be blessed in what he does.
James 1:25

Sweaty palms accompanied the butterflies that created havoc in my stomach as I sat at my desk trying to rally up enough courage to walk down the hallway to the principal's office. What had seemed so easy and right the night before as I shared my spiritual growth and conviction with my husband, now seemed like a Herculean task. Always the opportunist, Satan tried one last time to lure me into disobedience by giving me a brief overview of every doubt that he had presented to me in the last six months. Statements like, "You will not be anything if you do not have a professional career," "Your financial plans are going to be destroyed," and "What if God does not come through?" were overpowered by the undeniable knowledge that this was God's will whether I chose to honor it or not.

Wiping my hands on the soft, black material of my dress pants, I took a deep breath and rolled back in my desk chair. Memories of the students who had filled the room over the past two years flooded my mind as I rose to meet the spiritual challenge before me, and a blanket of grief enveloped my nerve-charged body as I slowly walked through the scattered desks toward the door. For a moment, I stopped and allowed the emotion to debilitate me while I dwelled on all I was about to give up. I loved this place, not because of what it was or where it was, but for what occurred here. Each day children gathered here to learn, giving me the awesome opportunity to make an attempt to fill in the blank spaces in their lives. Although not always successful, I gladly greeted the task, ready to do whatever it took to meet the needs of each child. I took a ragged breath and quickly expelled it as a sigh. An increase in the bustling activity outside my classroom door assisted me in redirecting my melancholy thoughts and forced me to face the task at hand. If I did not hurry, I would not be back before students started congregating in my room.

Reminding myself that God's plans for me were better than anything I could create of my own volition and refusing to entertain any thought other than ones that encouraged my progress across the room, through the doorway, and down the hall, I forced myself to put one foot in front of the other. I fought my way through the crowds of students who were sharing morning greetings on their way to breakfast. Cheerful greetings coming from rosy-cheeked, smiling adolescents were ignored as I continued my determined march down the hallway leaving confused students in my wake. As I neared the glassed-in area that served as the school's nucleus, nerves jittered all through my body, making me feel numb and tingly. Pressing my hand against the glass door that displayed the fingerprints of countless children, I sent up a quick plea for courage and peace as I stepped into the office.

Ringing phone lines and garbled requests from the

intercom system greeted me as I entered. Hoping to be the next to gain their attention, a disgruntled parent and a few students stood by the u-shaped counter that enclosed the secretaries' desks. Smiling sympathetically at the two women who rushed around attempting to manage the morning's onslaught of work, I bypassed the line and made my way to the short hallway that led to the principal's office. Seeing that the office door stood ajar, I tapped on it lightly with my shaking hands and peaked through the opening to see if he was at his desk. Sitting there in a crisp, white shirt and red, patterned tie, the principal waved me in as he wrapped up a conversation on the phone. My heart thudded in my chest as I sunk down into the plush chair that sat opposite from his desk. As I waited for the phone call to come to an end, I wondered if the statement that I would soon make would eliminate the relaxed smile that now graced the face of the man that sat before me. I did not have to wait long to find out, because just as the thought skittered across my mind, the principal cheerily said good-bye and rested the phone in its cradle.

Looking up at me expectantly, he maintained his chipper demeanor and inquired about my need. Hoping to minimize the shock that he was about to receive, I prefaced my statement by saying, "I have something to tell you that might be upsetting, so I hope it does not ruin your day." A look of concern crossed his face chasing away the smile that had been there moments before. At this juncture there was no turning back, so I plunged ahead with the little speech I had carefully prepared the night before. Sounding foreign to my own ears, my voice squeaked out small and shaky as I proceeded. "After a great deal of prayer, I have decided that I will not be coming back to teach next year. I believe God is telling me he has something else for me to do, and I have to be obedient even though I do not know what it is."

Silence filled the office for a few seconds while the principal tried to assimilate the words he had just heard. In a voice filled with doubt he asked, "Are you sure this is what you want to do?" The numb, jittery feeling continued to harass my body as I attempted to appear confident in my response while tears tickled at the back of my throat. "Yes and No. I know I do not want to give up teaching and the kids, but I know that I do want to honor God. Since the two seem to be attached in this situation, I have to obey God first and trust that he has a good and perfect reason for asking me to give up these things that are precious to me. I know that if I put teaching first I will miss out on something even better God has planned for me. I will miss out on his blessing if I am disobedient to his calling, and I am confident I do not want that to happen. As a result, I am sure that this is what I want to do."

With a resigned sigh he leaned back in the cushy desk chair and looked at me across the top of his cluttered desk. "Although I am sorry to lose you, I would never stand in the way of what God has asked of you. I have learned that doing God's will is the only thing in life that brings true happiness. Sometimes, we are tempted to put God off for something we have found that brings us enjoyment, but even those things lose their ability to bring joy when God is not in them. I wish you the best, and I know you will find what God has for you." We spent the next few minutes discussing the details of my resignation and the paper work that would need to be completed. Even though nervous energy continued to course through my being, an undeniable joy filled me up from head to toe.

Chapter Ten

(Summer 2004)

For God, who said, "Let light shine out of darkness, made his light shine in our hearts to give us the light of the knowledge of the glory of God in the face of Christ.
2 Corinthians 4:6

"There is no joy like that experienced when a person is serving God." From the look on the woman's face, it was evident that she was experiencing that same joy as she stood before her audience. Although no moisture found its way to her cheeks, there was a glassiness to her eyes that belied the onset of tears. Her voice was soft and husky with the love she felt for her Heavenly Father. "In that moment I discovered the key to the purest kind of joy that a human can experience. As humans, we often attempt to find joy through activities and the attainment of objects. Unfortunately, these pursuits only provide us with a cheap replica of that for which we are searching, and soon the events of life strip away the facade of contentment that we have wrapped ourselves in, leaving only the empty, gaping hole that has been superficially covered. Independent from the influence of environmental circumstances, this joy that I experienced was funneled into my soul by the hands of God. Nothing the world handed me could alter my state because it was controlled by my relationship with my Father in Heaven. Despite the unavoidable stressors that arose as a result of my resignation, God kept filling me with unexplainable jubilation and peace. By exercising my faith in an act of obedience, I allowed myself to enter into a type of blissful communion with God through Christ that cannot be duplicated through any other act."

Once again, she descended the stairs leading down from the podium. Only this time she gathered her notes and brought them with her to stand in front of the adolescent-filled pews. "I finished out that school year with great anticipation for what God had waiting for me in the future. God had always been faithful in the past, and he once again proved consistent. A smile gathered at the corners of her mouth as she relayed her next words to the crowd. "Of course, the tasks God had for me to do were a little shocking at first. While I caught myself fantasizing about some awesome feat God had for me to accomplish, he asked me to use my time to clean cabinets at my church and teach Sunday school instead. Although I must admit that these tasks were not ones I would have chosen on my own, I embraced them and found as much of an opportunity to love God through them as larger ones.

While I labored at these tasks, I realized that God was asking me to serve him in an additional way. He was once again asking me to share what he had taught me about himself. He wanted me to be obedient and share the great treasure I had found with others. You see, while experiencing all of the events I have shared with you today, I came to an understanding of who God is and who I am in him that has allowed me to experience the treasures of Heaven right here on earth in a way I have not been able to before. Through these events I came to the realization that God is a real, physical being that desires to be a part of my daily life, rather than a distant, spiritual icon. In addition, I have found that, when I submit to that desire, my soul is filled with love, hope, joy, and peace despite the circumstances that surround me. I have seen the worst of me being overcome by the best of him, and I am amazed by the power of my Creator to bring light into the darkness of my inner being." Any hesitancy brought on by nerves that had attempted to hang on since the beginning of the woman's presentation had been blown away by the passion that coursed through her veins and flowed out in her voice as she delivered these last words.

"In 1 Corinthians Paul says, 'For what I received I passed on to you as of first importance,' and he continues by telling the people he was speaking to about the amazing truths God had shared with him. I have a feeling God had directed Paul to share the treasures he had encountered in his relationship with his Father in Heaven in the same way he has directed me, so I want to let you know that today I have passed on to you the truths that God has pressed onto my heart in the hope that you will recognize, like I have, that they are of first importance in life.

Silence filled the sanctuary as her words sunk into the hearts and minds of the teens that sat before her. Knowing that she had been obedient in sharing her message and that the rest was up to God, she slowly made her way down the aisle to the doors at the back of the church. Behind her she heard the youth minister offer the opportunity to respond to the message in a soft, reflective voice, but the woman did not stop to assess the immediate results of her obedience. Pushing through the heavy, exterior doors that she had entered through only an hour before, she lifted up a silent prayer for the adolescents who had heard her message. Then, noticing that clouds had blocked the sun's warm rays from reaching the earth, she rejoiced as she was reminded of the ever-present light that warmed her soul.

See For Yourself

Although I hope that God has spoken to you through the words in this book, I want to emphasize that reading the Bible is the best way to learn God's truth. Use the following Bible studies to delve further into God's Word and the spiritual lessons you have encountered while reading this story.

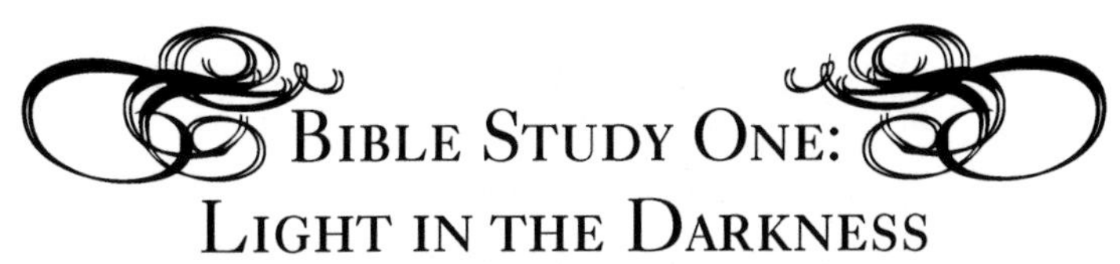

Bible Study One: Light in the Darkness

Throughout the Bible God is referred to or associated with light. Read the following scriptures:

Psalm 4:6
Psalm 27:1
Isaiah 60:19
Micah 7:8
John 8:12

People who encounter God experience his light. Read the following scriptures:

Exodus 34:29
Psalm 18:28
John 1:9
2 Corinthians 4:6
Ephesians 5:8

God originally intended for us to be in constant communion with his light, and as a result, our spirits would be continually lit from the inside, causing us to overflow with his glory. Unfortunately, sin got in the way. The Bible teaches us that sin separates us from God. The sad outcome of this is that we become disconnected from God's light, resulting in an internal blackout.

1. What do you think might be some consequences of this spiritual darkness?

We are blessed because God loves us so much that he decided to implement a rescue plan. In keeping with his just character, someone had to pay the punishment for the wrong that had been committed, so he sent Jesus to fill in for us. Although Jesus lived a sin-free life, basking in God's light, he chose to be separated from God on our behalf by taking on our individual sins.

Read Isaiah 53:4–5 and 1 Peter 2:24.

2. List some of the sins you have committed recently.

These specific sins were on Jesus that day on the cross, along with every other sin that ever has been or ever will be committed. Read *Matthew 27:46* and experience the moment that Jesus paid the punishment for them. Jesus experienced separation from God, not because of anything he had done, but because of our sins. He experienced the darkness for us, so we don't have to anymore. All we have to do is admit to God that we have done wrong things and tell him we want to accept the gift Jesus gave us on the cross. It is kind of like a rebate offer. The free gift is there, but you have to call in and ask for it. If you don't call, you don't get to take advantage of the reward.

What happens when you accept Jesus as your personal Savior? Well, you get reconnected with God's light. The separation that your sins deserve has been paid in full, so you can go on and enjoy the relationship that God always intended for you to have with him.

Read Galatians 5:13 and 1 Peter 2:16.

These verses warn us not to abuse the fact that our sins were paid for by Jesus. Yes, we are freed from punishment, but we should continue to express our gratitude to God by how we live our lives!

Are you lost in the dark? Ask Jesus to help you turn on the lights.

Bible Study Two: Set Apart

As Christians, we are to be set apart from the world by our behavior.

Read Romans 12:2.

God has given us an example, in Jesus, to show us how he wants us to relate to the world around us. Unfortunately, many Christians meld so smoothly with the world and its practices that no one can identify them as such unless they verbally identify themselves as a child of God.

1. Write the name of a Christian you know whose actions as well as their words attest to the fact that they are followers of Jesus.

What about this person's behavior is different from the kind of behavior the world promotes? Is there anything about this person's behavior that continues to conform to the world?

2. Do you think the people around you can tell that you have dedicated your life to God by the way you act?

What about your behavior is different from the kind of behavior the world promotes? Is there anything about your behavior that continues to conform to the world?

Most Christians would claim that their behavior sets them apart from the world. They do not steal or kill. They generously give to charity. They are always kind to the less fortunate in their community, and they are known to be trustworthy. This is an honorable set of qualities that definitely honor God, but are they enough to make the world recognize a difference in us? The answer is no. In fact, there are many individuals who do not know Christ and possess these qualities to some extent, so what does it mean to be set apart from the world? How can we live our lives in a way that honors God and communicates our love for him?

Read the following scriptures. Before you start, ask God to speak to your heart about what it means to be set apart from the world. After reading each verse, (1) write down God's view of the topic and (2) write the world's philosophy on the same topic. (3) Finally, compare the two and write down anything you feel God is teaching your heart.

Matthew 5:27

God's View______________________________________

____

World's View____________________________________

____

Matthew 5:38–41

God's View______________________________________

____

World's View______________________________________

____

Matthew 5:44, 46–47

God's View______________________________________

____

World's View______________________________________

____

Matthew 6:2–4

God's View______________________________________

____

World's View______________________________________

____

Matthew 6:19, 24

God's View______________________________________

____

World's View______________________________________

____

Matthew 6:25–34

God's View______________________________________

____

World's View______________________________________

____

Matthew 7:1–5

God's View________________________________

____

World's View________________________________

____

Ephesians 4:29

God's View________________________________

____

World's View________________________________

____

Philippians 2: 14–15

God's View________________________________

____

World's View________________________________

____

Look back at your answer for question 2. After reading these scriptures, do you feel the same? Do you see any areas of your life in which you have continued to conform to the world's philosophy?

You may feel a little discouraged right now. God may have convicted you on several counts as you read his Word and considered how it applied to your life, but do not lose heart. God loves you and accepts you just where you are in your Christian walk!

Read Philippians 3:12–15

A great Christian man, who loved God with all of his heart, yet he admits that he still makes mistakes, spoke these verses. Only God knew what Paul's spiritual shortcomings were, but I am quite confident they were similar to the ones we struggle with today: lusting, seeking revenge, disliking individuals who hurt us, being prideful and greedy, worrying about our future, overlooking the fact that we are sinners and condemning someone else with our actions or words, and complaining and arguing about things in our lives that do not seem fair. For this reason, Paul was able to give us godly advice about how to handle the mistakes we continue to make after we accept Jesus into our lives. He tells us to forget what is behind, knowing that we are already forgiven through Jesus' blood, and strain toward what is ahead. In other words, yes, I did dishonor God by the way I spoke to my husband this morning, but that is in the past. I realize it was wrong, but I also know that I am forgiven. As a result, I am free to make amends with my husband and do my best to honor God I the future.

In verse sixteen Paul states God's expectation for us in these areas of life that we have not yet mastered, "Only let us live up to what we have already attained." God is our individual spiritual tutor. He teaches our hearts his truths at different rates, and his expectations are based on what he knows we have learned. Our job is to continually seek his truth and wisdom and live up to what he has already taught us. If we do this, each day we will grow closer and closer to the person that he intended us to be.

What did God teach you today? Go, and live up to it!

Bible Study Three: Serving God

When choosing an area to serve God, we often focus on our abilities and talents as we make our decisions.

1. List some of your abilities and talents.

We want to find an area in which we are confident we will be of service, and we shy away from tasks that make us uncomfortable.

2. List some areas of service in which you would be uncomfortable because you do not feel you possess the necessary skills.

We go to the extreme of taking personality profiles and interest surveys in order to determine where we will be most useful. While there is nothing wrong with these tools, which can be helpful, they overlook one main detail in God's character.

Read 1 Corinthians 1:27–29

In the accounts recorded in the Bible, God does not often choose individuals to serve based on their most developed skills and abilities. In fact, he is shown as doing quite the opposite. Read the following Old Testament accounts of individuals God chose to do great things for him.

Exodus 3:10–12; 4:10–12 and Samuel 17:41–47

These are familiar stories, but we seem to have missed the point. God is trying to send us a message. He plans on using us in a way that will stun the world. What would be more awe inspiring: a great speaker persuading Pharaoh to let the Israelites go, or a man who readily admits that he is "slow of speech?" If the first man did the job, people would attribute the success to his great oratory skill and miss God's involvement, but if the second man did the job, it would be evident that his abilities had been greatly supplemented. God wants to make himself known, and he plans to use us, not just the characters in the Bible, to accomplish this task. For this reason, we need to be prepared to receive a call to serve in areas in which we are not skilled or comfortable, but we do not need to be afraid. We can trust God's promise to Moses, "I will help you . . . I will teach you . . ."

Read Matthew 25:14–30

Based on this parable it is obvious that God wants us to use our talents to honor him, but it is important to keep our heart in tune with his voice and not turn away from a specific calling that makes us uncomfortable because it is outside of our skill set.

Is God calling you to something that intimidates you? Trust him.

Bible Study Four: God's Word

As Christians, we believe that the Bible is God's flawless Word. Read the following scriptures:

Psalm 12:6
John 17:17
Galatians 1:11–12 1
Thessalonians 2:13
2 Timothy 3:16

As a result, we can rely on the words of the Bible to provide us with reliable guidance through any situation in life. If we are lost and confused or do not know how to handle the circumstances we are in, God's Word contains the answers that we need. There is no life event for which the Bible does not give guidance.

How often do you spend time reading the Bible?

What things keep you from spending more time studying God's Word?

What message do you think you are sending to God when you do not take time to read his Word?

The problem is many Christians do not know what God's Word says because they do not read it regularly. They depend on Sunday's sermon or the lessons in Sunday school to inform them of the wisdom contained in the pages of the Bible. As a result, they have an incomplete understanding of how God would like them the handle the events of life and the extent of his awesome promises. The Bible warns us that we should know what God's Word says for ourselves, so we cannot be deceived by cleverly crafted arguments that sound good but are not God's truth.

Read the following scriptures.

Colossians 2:2–3, 8
2 Corinthians 11:3–4

Do you feel like you know God's Word well enough to protect yourself against Satan's deception?

Read the following statements. All of them sound good, but one of them is not a truth from God's Word. See if you can identify it with your knowledge of the Bible.

Lend to your enemies without expecting to get anything back.

God helps those who help themselves.

No one can enter the kingdom of God unless he is born of water and the Spirit.

Bad company corrupts good character.

If you do not forgive others, God will not forgive you.

The point of this exercise is not to make you feel stupid or uneducated, but to emphasize how easily we can be deceived by statements and philosophies that appeal to our human understanding if we do not keep ourselves familiar with God's teachings. Number two is not a teaching from the Bible. In fact, such a statement might lead us to believe that God expects us be self-sufficient and try to make our own way in life in order to gain his support, which is completely contradictory to the Bible's teachings. Here are the Scripture references for the other statements: *(1) Luke 6:35 (3) John 3:5 (4) 1 Corinthians 15:33 (5) Matthew 6:14*

Another caution concerning Biblical use deals with the opposite extreme. Sometimes, we can get so caught up in gathering knowledge about the Bible that we miss the message in God's Word.

Read the following scriptures:

Matthew 13:14–16
Romans 2:13
James 1:25

The point of knowing God's Word is not to accumulate knowledge or to be able to impress the members of your Sunday school class. The purpose is to know God's will more clearly, so you can better express your love for him with your life.

What do you need to do so you can spend more time studying God's Word? Do it!

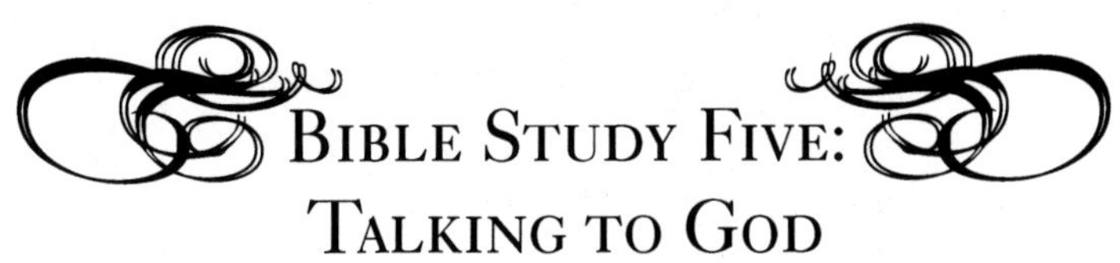

Bible Study Five: Talking to God

Praying is simply having a conversation with God. Unfortunately, many people are afraid to pray because they do not feel like they know how. There is a huge misconception that big words and lengthy oratory combine to make a conversation that is worthy of God's time. Here is what the Bible says about this idea.

Read Matthew 6:5–8 and Mark 12:40

God obviously does not give a hoot how impressive our vocabulary is or how many words we can chain together. He just wants to talk to us. He just wants us to want to talk to him. In fact, the Bible gives us permission to go so far as to groan to him. Read the following verses to get an idea of how desperately God wants to hear from us.

Romans 8:26
Ephesians 6:18
1 Thessalonians 5:17
Philippians 4:6
Colossians 4:2

Jesus did give us a sample prayer which you can find in *Matthew 6:9–13*. This prayer provides us with an outline and covers several topics that we need to regularly discuss with God: how great he is and how much we love him, our physical, spiritual, and emotional needs, the mistakes we have most recently made, and help to overcome our sin in the future. Does this mean that every prayer that we ever pray has to contain these elements or that these are the only things we can talk to God about? No, Jesus provided us with this example to guide us in our conversations with our Father in heaven, not to make them formal and uncomfortable.

So, let's practice. On a separate sheet of paper, write out your side of a conversation with God. Use normal, everyday language and communicate what is on your heart. Do not worry how it sounds or if the grammar is correct. Remember, God just wants to talk to you.

Now, you just wrote your side of the conversation. This leads us to another reason people do not pray. Read *2 Timothy 3:5*. A lot of individuals practice a form of religion but do not believe in God's power. For this reason, they feel it is a waste of time to talk to God because the conversation will be one-sided. Instead, believing they are self-sufficient, they attempt to fix their own problems and meet their own needs. This leads to all of the ungodly behaviors listed in verses 2–4.

Why do you think people might doubt God's power?

One reason might be that in the past they have prayed, and they did not feel like they received an answer. Read *Matthew 7:7–8 and 2 Peter 3:8–9*. How do you think these two verses apply to these individuals' prayer dilemma?

Read *James 5:16*. The last part of this verse says, "The prayer of a righteous man [or woman] is powerful and effective. This is a promise from God's Word. It is not a flippant statement. Read the following scriptures:

Romans 3:21–22
2 Corinthians 5:21
Philippians 3:9

These scriptures state that if you have accepted Jesus as your personal Savior, you have his righteousness; therefore, your prayers are powerful and effective.

Have you talked to God today? He's dying to hear from you!

Contact author Cori Lukomski
or order more copies of this book at

TATE PUBLISHING, LLC

127 East Trade Center Terrace
Mustang, Oklahoma 73064

(888) 361 - 9473

Tate Publishing, LLC

www.tatepublishing.com